D1117190

Presented to the Pasco
County Library System
In Memory of

Benjamin Hangun
Mower

Cultural Background

The Deer and the Woodcutter is a Korean folktale that has been handed down by word of mouth from one generation to the next. It has been told by grandparents to their grandchildren, huddled on the heated floors of Korean homes in the dead of winter, with the cold snow-laden winds raging outside; repeated in the yards of Korean homes to children seated on straw mats in the cool of a summer evening; and shared by farmer folk as they rested from their work in the fields in the shade of a nearby tree.

The author, Kim So-un, first heard *The Deer and the Woodcutter* when he was a child. He hopes that a wider audience will now enjoy this story, and that readers will feel a kindred spirit with the people of ancient Korea. Kim So-un is also the author of *Korean Children's Favorite Stories*.

Published by Tuttle Publishing,
an imprint of Periplus Editions (HK) Ltd,
with editorial offices at 153 Milk Street,
Boston, Massachusetts 02109 and 130 Joo
Seng Road #06-01, Singapore 368357

Illustrations © 2005 Jeong Kyoung-Sim
Text © 2005 Periplus Editions (HK) Ltd

LCC Card No: 2004110838
ISBN 0-8048-3655-8
First printing, 2005

Printed in Singapore

09 08 07 06 05 04
7 6 5 4 3 2 1

Distributed by:
North America, Latin America & Europe
Tuttle Publishing,
364 Innovation Drive,
North Clarendon, VT 05759-9436, USA
Tel: (802) 773 8930; fax: (802) 773 6993
Email: info@tuttlepublishing.com
Website: www.tuttlepublishing.com

Asia Pacific
Berkeley Books Pte Ltd,
130 Joo Seng Road #06-01,
Singapore 368357
Tel: (65) 6280 1330; fax: (65) 6280 6290
Email: inquiries@periplus.com.sg
Website: www.periplus.com.

Japan
Tuttle Publishing,
Yaekari Building 3F,
5-4-12 Osaki, Shinagawa-ku,
Tokyo 141-0032
Tel: (03) 5437 0171; fax: (03) 5437 0755
Email: tuttle-sales@gol.com

The Deer and The Woodcutter

A Korean Folktale

by Kim So-un
illustrations by Jeong Kyoung-Sim

TUTTLE PUBLISHING
Boston • Rutland, Vermont • Tokyo

Long, long ago, at the foot of the Kumgang Mountains, there lived a poor woodcutter. He lived alone with his mother, as he had not yet married. Every day he would go into the mountains to cut wood, as that was his job.

One fine autumn day, when the red maple trees flamed everywhere, the woodcutter went as usual to chop wood in the forest. Soon he was hard at his work. Suddenly a stately deer came running out of the forest. He was panting and seemed on the point of falling with exhaustion.

"Save me, please!" the deer cried. "A hunter is chasing me!" And he looked back in fear, expecting the hunter to come out of the woods at any moment.

The woodcutter felt sorry for the deer. "Here, I'll help you," he said. "Quick, hide under these branches."

The woodcutter covered the deer with a small tree he had just felled.

No sooner had he done this than a hunter appeared, carrying a gun.

"Say!" the hunter said. "Didn't a deer come running this way?"

"Yes," the woodcutter answered, "but he kept on going that way." The hunter quickly ran in the direction the woodcutter had pointed.

After the hunter was gone, the deer, who had kept completely still, came out.

"Thank you very much," he said. "You saved me from great danger. I shall never forget your kindness." The deer thanked the woodcutter many, many times and then disappeared into the forest.

4

Some days later the deer came again to where the woodcutter was working and said, "I have come today to repay you for saving my life. Do you wish to have a beautiful wife?"

The woodcutter blushed. "Of course I want a wife. But who would want to marry such a poor man as I?"

"Don't say that. Just listen to me. If you do as I say, you will be able to get a good wife this very day. All you have to do is ..." The deer put his mouth to the woodcutter's ear and began whispering. "Cross that mountain and go straight on, and you will come to a large pond. Often beautiful fairies come down from Heaven to bathe in that pool. They are sure to be there today. If you start now, you will be able to see them. When you get there, take just one of the robes which the fairies have hung on the trees while they bathe, and hide it carefully. Remember, take only one. Their robes are made of fine feathers, and without them the fairies cannot fly back to Heaven. There will be one fairy who will be left without her robe. Take that fairy home, and she will become your wife. Do you understand? Remember, take only one robe. You will surely succeed, so leave right away."

The woodcutter listened carefully, but it seemed like a dream, and he looked as if he did not believe the deer.

But the deer said, "Don't worry. Do just as you are told."

At this, the woodcutter decided to give it a try. As he started out, the deer called him back, "Oh, there is one more thing. After the fairy has become your wife, you must be very careful until she has borne you four children. No matter how many times she may ask, you must never show her the robe of feathers. If you do, there will be great trouble."

The woodcutter climbed straight up the path the deer had shown him. He crossed the mountain, and sure enough, eventually he came to a large pond. And in the pond he saw a number of fairies bathing, as beautiful as those painted in pictures. Hanging on the trees were many, many shining robes of feathers, as light and thin as the finest silk.

"So these are the robes of feathers the deer spoke about," thought the woodcutter. Quietly, he took one from a tree and folded it over and over. So fine was the robe that it folded into the thickness of a single sheet of paper. The woodcutter carefully hid the robe in his breast pocket. Then he sat down in the shade of a nearby tree and watched the fairies from a distance.

Soon the fairies finished bathing and came to put on their robes. Everyone had a robe to wear, all except one fairy. Her robe was missing. She looked everywhere, but it was not to be found. The other fairies were worried and they too joined in the search. They looked high and low, but the robe was nowhere.

After a long while, the sun began to set, and the fairies said, "We can't keep looking forever. The gates of Heaven will be closed. We will have to leave you here alone, but when we get back to Heaven we will talk with the others and try to do something to help you." Then they spread out their robes and flew up into the sky, leaving the one poor fairy all by herself beside the pond.

12

The fairy who had no feathered robe was finally taken home by the poor woodcutter and became his wife.

The two were very happy, and the woodcutter felt very lucky. Once the fairy had become his wife, she seemed to forget all about returning to Heaven, and eagerly worked in her new home. She cared faithfully for her mother-in-law and for her husband. Then one, two, three children were born to them, and she raised the children with loving care.

The woodcutter soon lost all fear that his wife might one day leave him.
His wife never once mentioned the robe of feathers, and the woodcutter never
mentioned it himself. But he still remembered the words of the deer, telling him
that he must never show his wife the robe until four children were born.

One evening after a hard day's work, the woodcutter was seated at home, sipping the drink his wife had served him with loving care.

"I never knew that Earth was such a pleasant place to live in," his wife remarked casually. "I wouldn't dream of returning to Heaven. But isn't it strange? I often wonder where my robe of feathers disappeared to. Could it be possible that you hid it?"

The woodcutter was an honest man at heart. So when his wife asked him about the robe, he couldn't bring himself to pretend ignorance. Besides, his wife had now borne him three children, and he could not lie to her. Also the food and drink had gone to his head, and he was caught off guard.

"I have kept it a secret until now," he said, "but you're right—it was I who hid your robe."

"Oh," she answered with a smile, "so it was you, after all. I often thought it might be so. When I think of the past, I feel a yearning for old things. I wonder how the robe looks after all these years. Please let me look at it for a moment."

The woodcutter felt relieved at having told his wife the secret he had kept hidden these many years. Forgetting all about the deer's warning, he brought out the robe and showed it to her.

His wife spread the beautiful robe in her hands, and as she did so, there stirred in her heart a strange and indescribable feeling. A snatch of an old song rose to her lips:

> The multicolored clouds now spread,
> Gold and silver, purple and red;
> And the strains of a heavenly sound
> In the balmy skies redound....

From the robe of feathers in her hands, memories of dreamy days lived in Heaven now returned so clearly, that she was filled with homesickness.

Suddenly she placed the robe on her shoulders. Then she put one child on her back and the other two under each arm.

"Farewell, my husband," she said. "I must, after all, go back to Heaven." And with these words she rose into the air.

The woodcutter was so surprised that he could not move. When he was finally able to run outside, his wife was high in the sky, looking like a tiny dragonfly winging its way to Heaven.

No matter how much the woodcutter
regretted his mistake, it was too late.

He no longer had the will to work. Every day he stayed
at home, staring into the sky, thinking of his wife and
three children.

One day the deer that he had saved came visiting. The deer
knew that the woodcutter's wife had returned to Heaven, taking
with her their children.

"Didn't I tell you?" the deer asked. "If there had been four children,
this would never have happened. You see, a mother cannot leave a child
behind. If you had four children, she could not have carried the fourth and
couldn't have left you."

When he heard this, the woodcutter felt even more ashamed of himself. All he could do was hang his head and continue sighing.

"But," the deer continued, "don't be too disheartened. There is still a way you can be reunited with her. You remember that pond, don't you? Since the day the robe was lost, the fairies no longer come down to Earth. Instead, they send down a bucket on a rope from Heaven and draw up water from that pond—it is believed this water is even better than the water in Heaven.

"Now, this is what you should do. Go to the pond and wait. When the bucket is lowered and filled with water, hurry and empty it out. Then climb inside the bucket and you will be drawn up into Heaven."

Once more the woodcutter did as the deer told him. And he really did get into Heaven. There he was able to meet his beloved wife and children.

His wife was once again a fairy, but she was overjoyed to see her husband and greeted him with open arms.

Many, many happy days followed for them. The woodcutter's life in Heaven was like a dream. Heaven was beautiful beyond belief.

Never had the woodcutter seen or even imagined such beautiful sights. Every day in Heaven was an ecstasy of delight.

But one thing troubled him. He often thought of his mother, whom he had left behind. Time and time again, he asked himself, "I wonder what Mother is doing now? She must be lonely, living all by herself."

And every time he thought of his mother, he kept saying, "If I could only see her just once, I would be very, very happy."

His wife, the fairy, said, "If you are so worried about her, why don't you go to see her? I'll bring you a heavenly horse, which will take you to Mother's place in a moment." So she brought him a heavenly horse.

As her husband was mounting the horse, the fairy said, "Listen! There is one important thing. You must never get off this horse. If you so much as set a single foot on the ground, you will never be able to return to Heaven. Whatever happens, you must stay on the horse."

Only after the fairy had repeated this instruction over and over again did she finally allow her husband to set out on his journey.

As soon as the woodcutter was firmly mounted, the heavenly horse whinnied once and was off like a bolt of lightning. In no time at all they reached the village of the woodcutter's birth at the foot of the Kumgang Mountains.

The aged mother had been very lonely living all alone. When she saw her son atop a horse at her door, she wept with joy.

But the woodcutter would not get off his horse. "Mother," he said, "I am so glad to see you well. Please take good care of yourself and stay strong and well forever. If I get off this horse, I cannot go back to Heaven, and so I must say farewell as I am."

After speaking to his mother, the woodcutter pulled on his reins and was about to set off for Heaven.

The mother was unhappy to part with her son. "You have come such a long way," she said. "How can you leave like this? If you cannot dismount, then at least have a bowl of your favorite pumpkin soup. I remember how you used to love it so. I have just made some, and it should be nearly ready now."

The mother went inside the house and soon returned with a steaming bowl of hot soup for her son. The woodcutter could not refuse his mother's kindness and took the soup bowl from her hand, still seated on the horse. But, what should happen? The bowl was so hot that the woodcutter dropped it as soon as it touched his hands.

The soup splashed all over the horse's back. The horse jumped with a start and reared back on its hind legs. The woodcutter was thrown to the ground. With a great neigh of pain, the horse leaped into the sky, leaving the woodcutter behind. In a twinkling of an eye, the horse was gone from sight.

Once again the woodcutter was left on Earth. But this time, no matter how he grieved and cried, it was no use—he could not return to Heaven.

Day after day the woodcutter lifted his face to the sky and called again and again to his wife and children. But it was too late. Even his friend, the deer, could no longer help him. Day and night the woodcutter yearned to return to Heaven. Day and night he yearned to see his wife and children again. And as he kept gazing up into the sky and calling to his loved ones year after year, he was slowly transformed into a rooster.

That is why, when country children today see a rooster atop a straw-thatched roof crowing out the time, they remember this story, told them by their grandparents, of the woodcutter crying for his wife and children.